When a Dad Says "I Love You"

Illustrated by

Douglas Wood   Jennifer A. Bell

Simon & Schuster Books for Young Readers

NEW YORK   LONDON   TORONTO   SYDNEY   NEW DELHI

To my dad, Jim, and my sons, Bryan and Eric,
who all taught me how to be a dad
—D. W.

For my dad, Roger
—J. A. B.

Acknowledgments
Special thanks to Kathy, always my "first responder,"
and to my editor, Julia Maguire, and artist Jennifer A. Bell,
who helped find just the right magic to bring this book to life.—D. W.

SIMON & SCHUSTER BOOKS FOR YOUNG READERS
An imprint of Simon & Schuster Children's Publishing Division
1230 Avenue of the Americas, New York, New York 10020
Text copyright © 2013 by Douglas Wood, Inc.
Illustrations copyright © 2013 by Jennifer Bell
All rights reserved, including the right of reproduction in whole or in part in any form.
SIMON & SCHUSTER BOOKS FOR YOUNG READERS is a trademark of Simon & Schuster, Inc.
For information about special discounts for bulk purchases, please contact Simon & Schuster Special Sales
at 1-866-506-1949 or business@simonandschuster.com.
The Simon & Schuster Speakers Bureau can bring authors to your live event. For more information or to book an event,
contact the Simon & Schuster Speakers Bureau at 1-866-248-3049 or visit our website at www.simonspeakers.com.
Book design by Chloë Foglia • The text for this book is set in Cochin.
The illustrations for this book were rendered in pencil and then finished digitally.
Manufactured in China • 0113 SCP
10 9 8 7 6 5 4 3 2 1
Library of Congress Cataloging-in-Publication Data
Wood, Douglas, 1951–
When a dad says "I love you" / Douglas Wood ; illustrated by Jennifer A. Bell. — 1st ed.
p. cm.
Summary: Explores some of the many and varied ways a father can express his love, even without saying the words,
such as by making pancakes, playing games, and reading a favorite story using special voices for each character.
ISBN 978-0-689-87532-8 (hardcover)
[1. Fathers—Fiction. 2. Father and child—Fiction. 3. Love—Fiction.] I. Bell, Jennifer A., ill. II. Title.
PZ7.W84738Wjg 2013
[E]—dc23
2012013268
ISBN 978-1-4424-5049-3 (eBook)

W hen a dad says "I love you,"
he doesn't always say it
in the plain old ordinary way.
That would be just a little bit . . . ordinary.

Instead he might just say . . .
"Rise and shine, Champ.
It's a great day!"

He might say "I love you" by making pancakes.
Even if they're a little bit . . . crispy.

Sometimes a dad says "I love you" by
feeling your mmm . . . your mmmusss . . .
There it is! Your muscle!

By helping you do a chin-up,
almost by yourself.

Or by racing you around the yard,
with only one stop for cookies and milk.

He can say "I love you" by playing here-comes-the-tickle-bug!

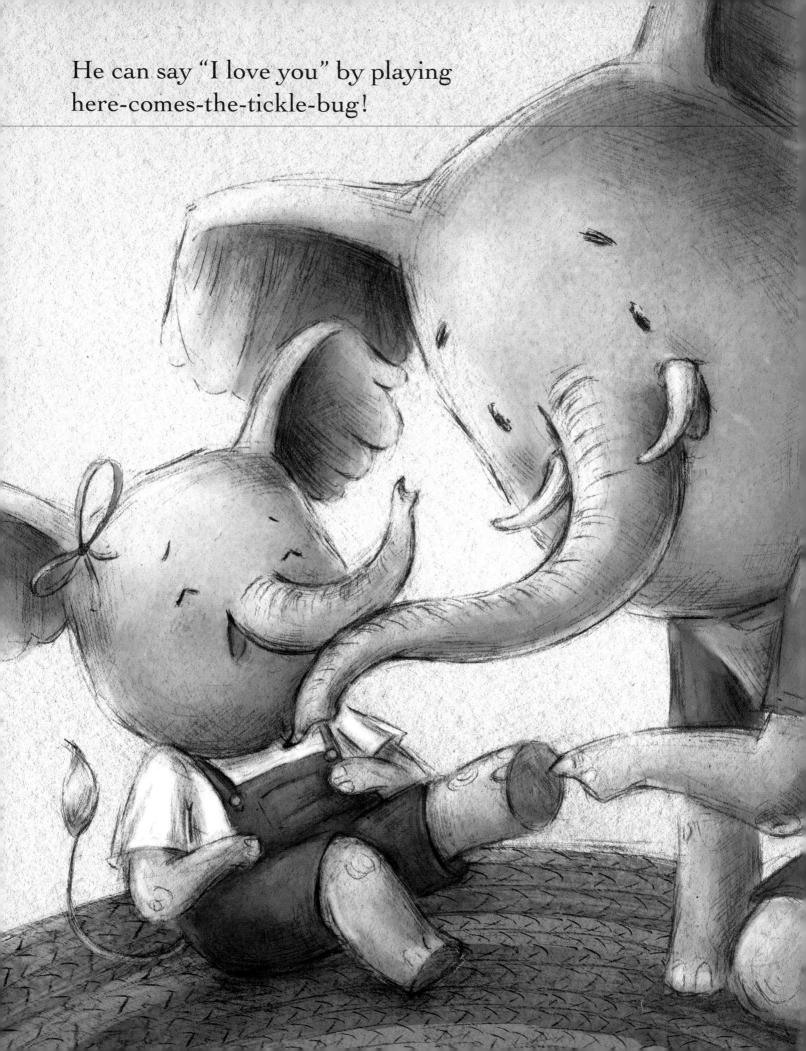

And by stopping . . .
just so you can catch your breath.

A dad might sing "You Are My Sunshine"
for the three hundred and sixty-ninth time
in one day.

He might call you silly names, like Mugwump or Snickle-fritz or Flap-doodle or Scatterwhomp!

Or he might just say,
"Don't worry—I've got you."

A dad can say "I love you"
by carrying you on his shoulders
just so you can see things better.

He can say it by doing all the rowing,
so you can catch all the fish.

He can say it by explaining what the world was like
when he was little,
and dinosaurs still roamed the earth.

And he can say it by answering all your questions,
especially the ones that start with "Why?"

A dad might say "I love you" by pulling a quarter out of your ear just so you can hear a little better.

He might help you with your homework,
even when he doesn't understand it.

He might show you the stars at night
and tell you all their stories.

And explain just exactly what
the moon is made of.

A dad might give you a bear hug,
and let you be the bear.

A dad can say "I love you"
by reading you your favorite story,
with voices for all the characters.
Again.
And again.

He can say it by carrying you up to bed
when your eyes won't stay open
and your legs won't work.

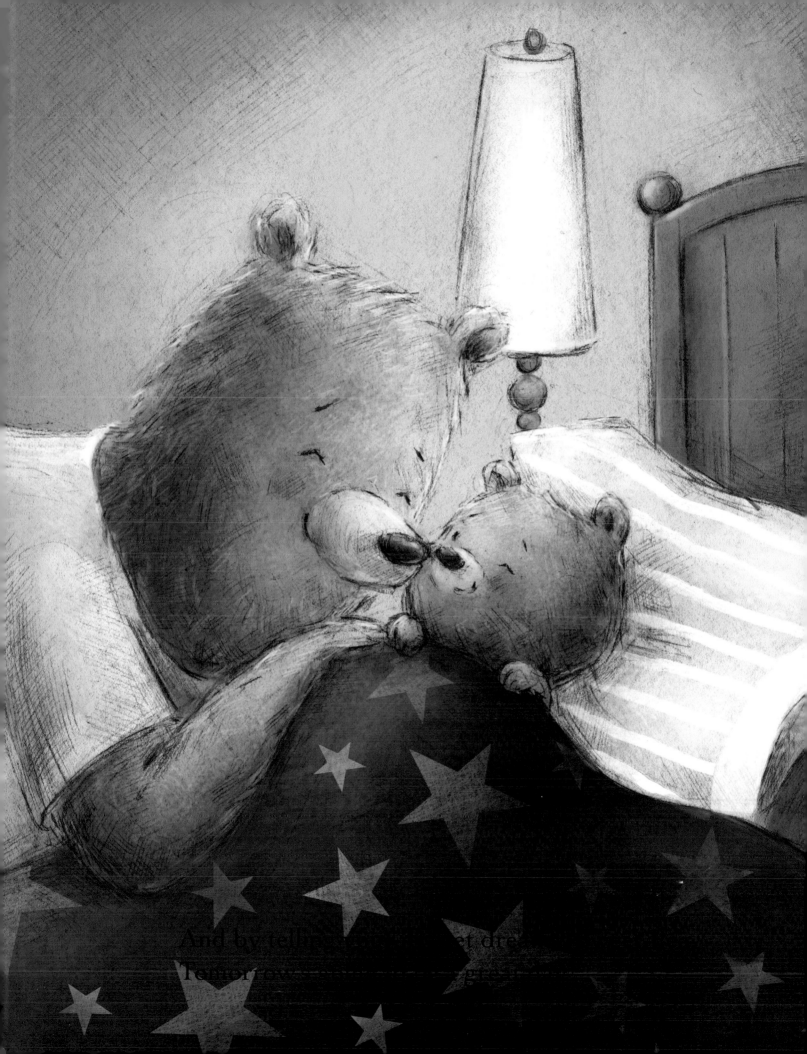

And by telling him that there is always
tomorrow.

And of course,
once in a while,
just to fool you,